sing me no more

sing me no more

◆ ◆ ◆

LYNNETTE DUECK

PRESS GANG PUBLISHERS
VANCOUVER

The Publisher gratefully acknowledges financial assistance from the Canada Council.

Canadian Cataloguing in Publication Data

Dueck, Lynnette, 1955 –
Sing me no more

ISBN 0-88974-046-1

I. Title

PS8557.U32S5 1992 C813'.54 C92-091584-1
PR9199.3D83S5 1992

First Printing September 1992
1 2 3 4 5 96 95 94 93 92

Editor: Barbara Kuhne
Cover and text design: Val Speidel
Cover photograph: Colette Leisen
Author photograph: E. Bradley Friesen
Typeset in ITC Stone Serif by The Typeworks
Printed on acid-free paper by Best Gagné Book Manufacturers Inc.
Printed and bound in Canada

Press Gang Publishers
603 Powell Street
Vancouver, B.C. V6A 1H2
Canada

To Beth, who helped me see the path,
to Rose, who helped me find it,
and to Brad, who walked it with me.

For a case of beer

For a case of beer and some cigarettes she sold her matching wedding band. That was what it was worth.

It will get me through this one night. Now when I need it. Now when the nights are hell.

They melt them down for their metal. It would vanish, disappear from existence, it would no longer match anything.

Fourteen bucks or twelve, she cannot recall. Cannot remember the cost of the beer.

It had not been her rock-bottom, melting the band for a case of beer, not hers. Rock-bottom had been all around her, round time like the face of a clock, before the marriage and after. After the separation and after the melt-down.

She had wallowed at rock-bottom for a time, for some time. Rock hit bottom while she lay beside her husband Jonathan on their bed and he refused her touch and she threatened to throw the banjo over the balcony, the hand-crafted magic banjo it had taken him years to pay for and that meant far more to him than she could ever mean. Longing to hear it smash. Shatter-break the deadly silence that mushroomed between them. Wanted to see it lying bent, twisted, mutilated. He would have noticed her then. Have killed her with his bare pacifist hands. But it would have broken that silence. The dead, dead, unbending silence. Vacuum of sucking silence. Vacuum of hatred.

Rock hits bottom.

The one everyone talks about is not the same as the one she has preserved in memory. The one she has makes her impotent. This is the heritage of her rock-bottom. This now.

✣ ✣ ✣

Drying out for

Drying out for the millionth time, her own private hell. That night-hell of barren prairie January that dragged her out through February and then March.

The boozers dried out and got on with the business of sobriety. They listened to the constant AA tapes, played cribbage, filled ashtrays while Nemah watched the twelve-year-old sniff-head disappear up the unused chimney. All she had were waves crashing against the walls of her brain.

The valium settled a blanket over Nemah. The stelazine made her eyeballs retreat into her skull, her neck snap rigid without warning, froze her in her tracks. She had seizures and convulsions, they could keep it.

She checked herself out of that centre, dropped out, walked away. She lacked focus. She lacked commitment. She lacked recoverability. She moved for some time through the fog-cloud where sights and sounds washed across her brain without sense or sequence.

Nemah lies on a bare mattress on the floor of some bedroom where she has at one time paid rent. The sheet around her body has not been washed in months, maybe since she moved in, she cannot recall. It is a wedding sheet. There is dried vomit on the pillow, traces of dried blood on her face. She cannot remember.

She opens her eyes and wonders why she is still alive. No thinking today. Sits slowly and examines her body, she knows there will be fresh bruises. This is the ritual morning mystery time. Who the fuck is she?

WHO. THE. FUCK. AM. I. WHY. AM. I. STILL. ALIVE.

Toilet is real, that porcelain bowl she hugs as the puke spills out, is this rock-bottom? First, whatever it was she drank last night, and then the familiar bitter green bile. Sometimes there is blood.

The Holy One from upstairs stands by Nemah's bathroom door—who let her in?—she yells like some fishwife.

WHY. ARE. YOU. DOING. THIS. TO. YOURSELF. NO. SELF. RESPECTING. MOTHER. WOULD. ACT. THIS. WAY. YOU. ARE. DESTROYING. YOURSELF. YOU. ARE. DISGUSTING. YOU. LIVE. LIKE. A. PIG. DISGUSTING. VILE. PIG. HAVE. YOU. NO. DECENCY.

GOD KNOWS I'M TRYING, Nemah spits out. GET THE HELL OUT OF MY BATHROOM.

✣ ✣ ✣

lost track

She has lost track of time in her no-valium fog. Somewhere along the track, while still pretending to be alive, she had beer and now she does not.

Bernie from the Centre graduated sober and got his certificate and graduation marble. A success. Bald. Fringes of greasy hair around that. Short. He gets beer.

A bed so enormous that it touches the wall on three sides and Nemah has been tied to it. Somehow. Naked. The projector Bernie has cleverly camouflaged begins to project against the wall at the foot of the bed and then there is "Debbie Does Dishes."

Debbie bigger than life with no escape and that ugly little man pulling on himself and panting and then he isn't there and then he is. She is in a time warp, a warp of time, captive and staring at those bizarre images at the foot of her prison.

After Debbie does dishes she does something else and then something else and the weird little Bernie seems to have an endless supply of Debbie doing stuff. There is no escape from Debbie doing. After Debbie there come other doings like mutilations and decapitations and Nemah wishes Debbie would return to do more dishes.

She pukes. Right there in that prison, careful not to swallow, raising her head high and spitting. Because she does not want to asphyxiate right there with Bernie the marble-graduate of sobriety jerking himself off as though she does not exist.

She hears him chatting to someone in the other room.

When she comes to, she has been released from her bonds. She calls.

"Bernie," she says.

She finds her clothes crumpled in a clump on the floor. No Bernie. Gone to work most likely, he sells cars for a living, it must be a pretty good living. A marble-graduate, some credential.

There is an open case of beer in the living room. She takes it with her. She has earned it. Every drop. Every last drop.

✣ ✣ ✣

boxes

Mostly Nemah keeps her boxes tightly shut. Most of the time. Most of the time, life can be carried out of just one box. Sometimes less. She can live for some time from nothing, from void. No history, no memory, no mementoes. Things just tie her down, hold her in bondage like four solid walls. Like doors and windows, furniture. Like children.

Boxes sealed and secure. Nemah's boxes filled with hard, sharp memories.

Keeps those monsters at bay. Tucks them away.

But she carries all of them with her wherever she goes.

❖ ❖ ❖

scared of the Man

Nemah is scared, scared, scared of the Man. Tries to find some teeny-tiny hiding hole where only she can fit. Wobbly like jelly inside. Stuff in her mouth like vomit, feels sick.

The Man will come and no one will help because he is boss, next to God.

She burrows way under her bed into the darkest corner, she is all squeezed in. There is dust. House is still. For now.

Thunder. Her name. Yelled.

"NEMAH!"

I wish I was dead.

"NOW!"

If I was dead then they couldn't.

Thunder. House shudders.

If I was never even born.

And after all it is easy, simple, shoves the bed and there she is.

Stupid, why didn't I know that?

GET. OUT. OF. THERE.

Not words but white flames shooting from hollow face of Father. Not any more real than cement or tombstones. And she moves out of her own free will, is not dragged. Stands (dead) on her own. two. feet. And marches out of there ahead. Down the stairs to that cold grey basement.

If never even born.

Stiff, she cannot speak, all sound is dead. Jaw would splinter if forced to open.

WHAT. CAN. YOU. SAY. FOR. YOUR. SELF.

Nothing, I can't.

ARE. YOU. SORRY.

Don't.

Save this humiliation for later, and the anger. Leather stings, whistles, and then she cries. Because.

There is no way out, no way, no way.

In that basement there is a grey monster named Furnace. She knows even at age four because she is smart-as-a-whip. Down those steps she fell once and smashed open her head on that cement. This basement is saved for only dirty grey stuff. Like her.

This is not the worst but part of the beginning of the worst.

⁂

counted spackles

Nemah lay in bed, counted spackles on the ceiling above. Green and yellow rose stems twisted down the wallpaper to the baseboards and caught in the crack between the door and the wall.

One glowing narrow eye, one enormous hairy toe. Nemah blinked rapidly to erase the monster there.

The monster is in my closet.

Her father's sudden snore chased the monster back.

That snore has a power all its own, it can make the monster vanish. Father's snore.

The monster is in my head, it is all just made up inside my brain.

Brother was not yet home but father was sleeping, snoring to wake the dead.

Good. No noise tonight. Unless that snore stops.

Brother will return. He will be drunk but he will tiptoe down the stairs softly to his bedroom. Listening for Father's snore. Nemah will watch the sky pinken and listen for her brother's stealth.

I am the keeper of the night, I am the dawn-keeper. Without me, something might happen. Something will surely happen.

If I should die before I wake.

Nemah has trouble sleeping at night, a thing which she keeps to herself. It is her own well-kept secret.

If she told, there is no saying what might be done. There might be medicines. There might be pills. There might be swattings. Anything might have already been invented to protect her from being the night-keeper. There is no telling what form her protection might take.

✣ ✣ ✣

Keepers

Keepers of the night are given potions to subdue the senses, fall in line, to accept the night, the monsters, and the closet doors.

Father's snore means safety.

Mother never sleeps, prowls like some night-beast. So she says, but Nemah knows better. She sleeps, and when she does, others prowl and devour.

Push it away, push.

By the time Nemah has words, the night monsters have gone.

With time and words, she begins to think they never were. Thinks it was all some dream.

⌖ ⌖ ⌖

That ugly

That ugly brown leather strap, Nemah could not look at it. It was so ugly she squeezed her eyes shut. He could not make her open them.

Her humiliation burned hot behind her face-skin.

Oh, not on the bare bum.

✣ ✣ ✣

make herself fly

Swing and swing and swing.

Nemah's feet kick up high, into the blue, blue sky. Swing, swing, she pushes herself away from the dirt below, the garden, the green, green grass, pushes hard and fast. Maybe she can make herself so high she will disappear. Maybe make herself fly.

Kicks up her toes and pushes frantically.

Ahead is the white-painted garage with red-tiled roof. Ahead is that proud new bungalow, also white with red. Behind is the garden, black dirt, green different shades, plants row upon row. Behind all that is forest, uncut brush, raw wild growth.

Pushes, her abdomen presses out, collapses, refills with great gulps of free air. Above there are clouds white and pillowy in china blue sky. Up there are birds. Up there is away. The only escape except for down and dirt.

Nemah pushes away from the dirt, the house, the garden.

This is as far away as she can get from them without being disobedient. Without leaving the yard.

Nemah's mother is hanging out wash on the long clothesline. The laundry flaps softly. Her mother wears a white apron that covers her wash-day dress. Her hair is messy.

She doesn't look at Nemah. Doesn't notice. Good, she is safe for now. She will not get into trouble if no one can see her.

✣ ✣ ✣

Sundays

"Ju-hust as I ah-ham withou-hout one plea," sang the people. "Oh La-hamb of Go-hod I come . . . "

Little Nemah shuffled her feet, kicking the rhythm with the heels of her polished shoes on the back of the pew. Her mother glared. Nemah stopped kicking and played with her Bible. Its pliant red leather cover felt soft and smooth in her hand. She flipped it open and turned the pages rapidly until she found the picture. Snakes. Snakes were writhing out of the man, slithering, slimy, they crept along the page. One's face stuck over the edge of the picture. Yucky. She slammed the book shut. Her mother glared at her some more.

She twisted her hanky between her forefinger and thumb and then watched as it untwisted itself. She tried to form the hanky into a baby in a cradle the way some of the old women could do, but she didn't have the knack of it yet. Those old women never bothered to teach her how, they did it quick as a wink and handed it back for her to play with. She did not play with it, she undid it to try to figure out how it was done. A hanky did not keep folds in it the way that paper did, which was how she figured out paper airplanes.

At long last, the minister asked the people to rise for the benediction and then she could talk again with no glaring. There was only calm talking inside the church so Nemah got out of there fast. She screamed around the parking lot with the other freed kids until their families were all done with chatting and gossip and were ready to leave.

Everyone crammed into family cars to drive back to their houses, even though they all lived close, in town, except for farm kids.

Every Sunday, Nemah begged to go somewhere. Sundays were lousy, with sleeping parents and nothing much to do because all Saturday chores had been done the day before. Kids in the country could at least play outside, run and scream around, that was for school yards not for where civilized people lived.

Church-day Sundays. Holy Sundays.

Every Sunday before they left for Sunday school, Nemah's father made the big beef roast ready so by the time they got home there would be dinner.

The house smelled heavenly. And that roast gravy was the best there ever was. It was almost worth it to have to sit through church.

Right when they got home from church, they all took off their good clothes and then the kids helped to set the table and get the dinner on. Best dishes and silverware, trays and gravy boats, tablecloth nice but covered with clear plastic in case of spills. Nemah loved that stuff. Also for best there were cut glass salt and pepper cellars.

For everyday there were the ordinary boring plates and cutlery, mismatched everything, missing cups and sloppy. But for the Day-of-Rest there were delicate things with no melmac or tupperware that tasted gummy-old.

Certain things were allowed on God's favourite day. Nemah wanted there to be perfect days all the time, and all the time she whined about that. Her brothers and sisters made fun, she being youngest and everyone else older and smarter and better at you-name-it.

Except for the special dishes, Sundays ended up pretty boring with not much to do. Sunday evening there was another church-going which was better because it was shorter and less holy. There were little skits and often Nemah would sing alone or with sister, songs that had to be practised. Words had to be right and melodies too.

Nemah liked to be singled out and liked how the old people said after how pretty she had sung.

Once Nemah forgot her words, standing there on the stage like stone, mouth dry, mind blank. Nothing, nothing.

"Somebody help me," she prayed. "Give me these words."

Faces staring, staring, made of cement.

WHAT IS WRONG WITH THAT CHILD IDIOT CHILD WHY HAS SHE STOPPED SINGING WRONG WRONG WRONG IDIOT

Oh God.

After a century, Daddy got up, came close to Nemah, whispered those words but she was stone-deaf from embarrassment.

What?

He repeated them.

What?

Then at last he said those missing words out loud and Nemah heard and finished the song. One thousand deaths later. One thousand deaths.

Those old people still grinned and said "good singing," so it made no difference after all. Just a song after all.

But not to Nemah. Not to her. To her, there were no small things. None in the world. Not in the whole entire world were there any small things.

Not to Nemah.

⁂

Don't let me die

"Don't let me die," she pleads, not wanting to give God the option.

At night she is scared to fall asleep because she knows she is one evil, wilful child and even kids can die, and if she is one of them, He will send her straight to hell and eternal damnation. Then there will be no more chances to try to be good.

Sister bows her head—all of them do, the whole row of girls and women in white on one side, boys and men in black on the other. Each bows while Preacher walks solemnly along the line pouring water on heads. Nemah strains to see but can't. Too many big people all around in the way.

She shivers as that same old silly goose prances over her grave, shivers again thinking of it. It is too cold in this church. Windows way high do not allow for sunlight.

Sister is goody-two-shoes. Doesn't need any help getting into heaven, she was just born good. Everybody knows that. Not like Nemah who was born rotten to the core.

Sister wears white like for a wedding but this is no wedding. She got her hair done up at the hairdresser's on Main Street. Maybe some of that Holy Water will spill over on her made-up face or that pretty too-white dress. Nemah wants to giggle but this is sacred so she is not allowed a laugh.

Sister is Daddy's little girl, she lives in his hip pocket. She lights him up like a Christmas tree but she is a complete stranger to Nemah.

Maybe she will die.

Nemah cranes her neck to see around the shoulders of the people in front of her, wants to see that Holy Ghost poured over that neat-as-a-pin hairdo. Wonders if some blessed liquid light will spill over.

Maybe only the Good can see.

✣ ✣ ✣

about your mother

"How do you feel about your mother?" The doctor's pursed lips formed puckers and pockets in creases around his mouth.

Nemah wondered about kissing that mouth. Soft. It would be soft and furry like a navel maybe. Round and empty inside. She willed herself to think about the question but the desk phone buzzed and he turned immediately away.

"Excuse me for a minute," he said politely, not looking at Nemah. "Hello?"

She watched his lips move and thought about the words.

Mother. Feel. Mother.

She had outlined it all for him, had tried to chronicle it in linear sequence. It might make more sense to him than it did to her.

"I'm sorry for the interruption," he said, pencilling random notations on a pad beside the notebook he used for her. For her case. "Where were we?"

He glanced at the open notebook. Apparently he was lost. Nemah waited patiently.

"You were saying?" he asked finally.

"You asked me about my mother," she said.

"Ahhh yes, mother. How do you feel about that?"

She did not have a script, all she had was some life to show him.

"Well, she's a mother," said Nemah carefully. She sensed a trap.

"*Your* mother," he reminded.

She leaned forward, trying to read the notes about her upside down.

"Do you believe in reincarnation?" she asked, leaning back. She could not read those turkey scratches even right-side-up. "Can I smoke in here?"

The doctor removed some coloured plastic-covered paper

clips from a delicately pearled shell, then slid it across the oak veneer desk.

"Use this," he suggested.

Nemah extracted a cigarette with shaking hands.

"Why did you cut off all your hair?" he asked.

"I was sick of it. It made me sick," Nemah said. The lighter flickered and died in her hand. She relit and inhaled. "Don't you like it?" she asked.

"It's very short. Isn't it tough to cut it by yourself?"

"I fucked it up," she whispered. Leaned forward and squinted at the doctor through her smokescreen. Skeletal smile. "Let's talk about sex instead," she said.

✣ ✣ ✣

Mother's room

Mother's room held some of Nemah's most favourite things. Like a big polished walnut dresser shiny like patent leather and on the dresser a silver-handled brush with bristles as soft as a newborn kitten which Nemah was not allowed to have in their house. Also in silver, a mirror. In it Nemah's whole face reflected and was caressed by silver.

✣ ✣ ✣

A muscle relaxant

The doctor scratched some words on a prescription form and passed the paper to Nemah.

"This should help," he said.

She studied the black scratches carefully.

"What is this for?" she asked finally.

"A muscle relaxant," he said. "It will help with your insomnia and the tension."

Nemah grinned and gently folded the slip into four sharp corners.

"Thanks," she said.

She tucked the paper inside the tight coin pocket of her jeans and stood.

"I'd like to see you on Thursday," he said. "Make an appointment at the desk."

⯎ ⯎ ⯎

The prescription

The prescription safe in her pocket, Nemah glanced at the doctor.

"This is easier," she said. "I mean it. You'd never believe some of the tricks I've had to pull."

She had always known there would be something. Some protection against being the night-keeper.

❖ ❖ ❖

Suck on that babe

"Suck on that babe, that's it. Bottoms up, good girl."

Nemah wiped at her mouth with the back of her hand.

"Like that?" she asked.

"Great, do that again."

She took the tumbler.

"Do it again," he said.

Bitter saliva mingled with sweet blood behind her tongue.

"Wait," she said, "just a second."

He thumbed at the pills on the table. Nemah touched the tumbler to her lips and drank.

"There's a good girl," he said.

"I hate scotch," she said. "I'm going to puke."

"Scotch makes you hot," he said thickly, pushing the heel of his hard hand against her crotch.

"I mean it, I have to puke," she said.

He unzipped his jeans.

"Look," he commanded.

"Oh Christ," Nemah muttered.

Above her, he rose. Shoving.

"There," he said. "Shit, you're great."

Dry inside, she scratched him like sandpaper.

When she returned from the bathroom, he was sifting through the pills.

"These are yours," he said. "Tens and fives. That should keep you for awhile. You can come back next Tuesday."

He had rearranged the cushions, everything seemed normal. Nemah scooped the tablets quickly into her bag. Sometimes he changed his mind. Sometimes he took them back. She had to move fast. A good girl, or he would take back her reward.

"Thanks," she said, opening the door, pulling her coat tight.

"Tuesday," he said absently, fingering his pills.

✣ ✣ ✣

smoke reefer

Source and Pat and Sybil and Nemah smoke reefer in Pat's parents' house. Pat cranks up the stereo loud, every tone is crystal as a frosted heartbeat.

Later, they all lie on the lawn in the back yard and peer at the sky, watch the clouds change shape, collect together and stick. Wisp and vanish.

Source tells about their love, their dreams, says to Nemah what life will be like for them together and she sinks deep into his words.

Then they make love.

Nemah knows she is all his forever.

"You belong to me," he says. "All mine you are."

"Yes," she says.

She will do anything.

time in cars

Source and Nemah spend a lot of time in cars. Parked cars or driving, drinking or smoking, there is no other place in this nowhere town to party. Everyone does it. Fuck in cars, smoke dope, argue. Wheels. Freedom. Parents cannot see inside cars.

Source has a bunch of new friends from the city. This one hairstylist he likes and wants Nemah to be more like, she is nothing more than pretty, talks about make-up and plays pool. She doesn't think about everything the way Nemah does. She is not depressing. Not like Nemah.

There's five of them drinking and toking, driving around. Source sits in the middle of the back seat. On one side, there is Nemah, on the other is the Stylist. Source's one hand rests on Nemah's leg. An open Labatt's between his thighs, she reaches for his other hand. Can't find it and then she sees. It is on her. On the Stylist. Nemah's stomach churns and she feels like puking.

What is he doing, what does he think he is doing?

The car has stopped so someone can take a piss at the roadside and Stylist gets out to stretch her muscular legs or something. Nemah hears her laughing.

"What are you doing?" she asks.

"I don't know what you're talking about," Source answers smugly.

"Touching her," says Nemah. "Why?"

"Never mind," he says, "mind your own business."

"You want to do it with her. Right here with me beside. Watching."

"You're imagining," he says, "there's nothing."

Stylist returns. Source slides an arm along the back ledge behind her. Nemah jerks herself away from him and leans her cheek against the window cool with air-conditioning. Her belly heaves. Keep it inside, she tells herself, we'll soon be home.

❖ ❖ ❖

none of your business

Lana marks the seat behind Nemah in language arts class.

"What happened to your face?" she whispers.

Nemah slides into her desk, turns slightly.

"I hit it on the cupboard door," she lies.

"Yeah right," mutters Lana, "same door."

"That's right," Nemah snaps. "Same fuckin' door."

She shimmies front and flips open her textbook. *Black Like Me.* It is what they are studying this month.

"Ya gotta stop bein' so fuckin' clumsy," says Lana loudly.

"Shut up," Nemah hisses. "It's none of your business."

Nemah tries to fill in both seats beside her in biology class but when Source shuffles in late, he tells the silent girl to her right to shove over and he sits. Snaps open his textbook, his binder. Glares at her. Leans close.

"Bitch," he spits in her ear.

She shifts her chair slightly away to the left. He grabs at her hand under the table.

"Bitch," he repeats. "What's wrong with you anyway?"

She tugs, trying to loosen his grip. Oh Christ, not here.

"What?" she asks.

"Why are you ignoring me?"

"What?" she says.

Teacher begins biology and Source twists his palm around her fingers. Starts to bend them slowly back. Tears spring to her eyes and she blinks. He bends, bends, bends until her fingers are pressed as far back as they can be.

His dark hair blends with her fair, bent together over the book on the table.

"What did I do?" she whispers. "At least tell me."

"Fuckin' bitch, you know."

She is still trying to free her hand and finally she does, the teacher has asked Source a question. She makes her escape from the classroom coughing, long hair forward to hide her face, she runs to the ladies'.

She will wait for him though after class and there will be hell to pay for this premature release. This is part of the cost of the abortion but that damage has been done and cannot now be undone. It cannot be unaborted.

✣ ✣ ✣

God is Love

"God is Love," the Sunday school teacher told the class.

"Why does He make people hurt so much then? From love?" asked Nemah.

Teacher had no answer, just blank verses from the Bible.

"I think it is all stupid," said Nemah. "I think God is dumb."

Teacher kicked her out of Sunday school.

"Don't come back till you apologize," she said.

"To whom?" Nemah asked.

❖ ❖ ❖

Washed in the blood

"Washed in the blood, in the wonderful blood of the lamb."

The congregation warbles, church building full to overflowing for Revival. Everyone has come to hear this preacher, this man of the golden voice tell about sin.

Little Nemah shivers when he talks.

"Whether or not you know it, you are all sinners," he says, and the choir chorus hums behind his voice like angels.

Nemah feels her spirit black as Satan.

Sinner.

"Sinner come home. Even you at the very back of this church, even you with hardness in your heart. Dear brother, dear sister, Jesus can fill you up, take away that despair, make you clean again."

Choir chorus hums louder, ready to burst into song.

Clean.

Clean again.

Angels call to Nemah, tug at her, she rises with the congregation to sing.

"I have to go forward," she whispers to her big sister.

Sister prods her waist encouragingly.

Nemah clutches her little red Bible, her legs feel like marshmallow, weakly she forces herself to move. She is so scared, she thinks she will pee her pants.

At the front, there are others like her, other sinners hearing the call of Jesus.

In a dream, the congregation leaves the church.

She is stuck standing at the front.

Preacher holds up his hands, Bible clenched between them, raises his face to the heavens.

Nemah gazes at the wood beams up there, imagines she sees Jesus floating.

She thinks she is supposed to feel something, this is supposed to make her feel different. Something different than just more scared.

Preacher prays over them, Nemah remembers the whole family is waiting. Her brother will be laughing. Stupid Nemah. Dumbest little kid.

Luckily people are still milling around, she is not the last one out. The family in the car says nothing. Her father starts the engine and drives them home.

After she has crawled into her bed, her mother comes. Sits.

I am in deep trouble now.

"You are Saved now," Mama says. Her voice sounds tired, tears are in it.

Nemah is silent. This is always her best defence.

"You will have to pray for God to make you good," says Mama. "This tonight in itself is not enough. It is only one small beginning. Prayer and asking forgiveness is next, you must confess all your sins."

To whom, Nemah wonders. The sins she has, she cannot say. They would beat her more, maybe even kill her if they knew the half of it.

"Yes," she says meekly.

"Tell me," says Mama.

"I have to think," says Nemah.

No more salvation can be found. Not if it means this. Besides, it's not enough.

Nothing is ever enough.

✣ ✣ ✣

Runs away

Runs away from home at thirteen, again at fourteen.

Every time she runs, they track her down with police.

There is no escape. She does not understand the trick to staying lost.

✣ ✣ ✣

and being sixteen

A sultry hot June afternoon, Nemah and Source lying together on the sand wearing as little as necessary. Sun beating against bared skin, so much skin exposed, and being sixteen.

Source's fingers crept underneath Nemah's bikini bottom and pressed and pressed there. She spread her legs, nibbled his earlobe.

"I wanna lick you here," he said, his voice sandy.

She smoothed her palm down his back, sliding fingers under where fabric began, she touched his body.

"Do it," she said, arching.

"Here?"

All around the beach was littered with bodies. Kids, old people, all getting hot.

"Here," he said. "I don't think so."

Nemah giggled. "Right here," she said. "Anyone could see."

"They'll kick us off. This is a public beach."

"Let's," she said, tongue flicking against his teeth.

She raised the grainy blanket and he rose over her, trunks peeled back. Gulls screeched overhead where she could watch them. Sun beat and joined them with squeaky sweat.

"What are you kids doing?"

Uniform. Oh shit.

"Nothing," panted Source.

"Well you can't do that here," snapped Uniform. "This is a public place. Get yourselves some privacy if you can't control yourselves."

Source flopped to her side, careful to keep the blanket around.

"There are families here, with little kids. Smarten up, you two."

Uniform disappeared.

Couldn't keep their hands off each other, the pleasures of their skin.

She left school after the abortion to become a live-in babysitter in the city. They gave her a room in the attic. She did dishes and swept and cleaned the bathroom while the mother sat and sat, watching the new baby. She did not allow Nemah to touch that baby.

The baby's father, Simon, took her for a drive one night. The car ended up on the old landfill hill where Simon told her to go down on him. Unzipped his pants and there it was, hairy and stubby, she did not want to touch that.

"In your mouth," he said pushing, "or I'll tell her and she'll make you leave tonight."

He had a flabby belly under old-man pants.

She did what he said, it did not take long. He drove her back to the house. Nemah waited until the weekend, then she packed her bags and did not return.

"Have you ever fucked anyone besides me?" demands Source.

She cannot answer. Thinks it counted.

"Have you?" he says. "Have you?"

"No," she says finally, too late.

"Who?" Source asks. "Tell me who."

"No," she insists, "no I never."

Guilty, I am guilty as sin.

✣ ✣ ✣

passion purple

The bedroom of their apartment where Source and Nemah are playing house is painted passion purple from the back shelves of some dusty hardware store. Clearance colours. Close your eyes and see purple. See purple all night long.

Their creepy caretaker pokes around their stuff while they are gone. Once Nemah pretends to be asleep after Source leaves for work and she hears the key turn the tumblers. The man creeps in, doors and drawers open and softly close, Nemah squeezes shut her eyes under the blanket and holds her breath. She thinks she hears him rummage in her underwear drawer.

At the Safeway where they shopped, Source and Nemah rummaged for treats.

"Bananas," he decided. "You choose."

And then watched her touch their stems.

Cream cold inside her, creamy cold. Source sucked some off her nipples, little boy nipples, she arched her back. Begging. He slid in two fingers and she bit herself against them, clenched them inside herself. Cold. Hot.

"How does that feel?" she asked, wanting words.

"You feel," he said, and she did.

"Mmmmmm," she hummed, "steamy. Slippery."

He peeled a banana as she felt herself. "Here," he said.

She pushed. "Dessert," she said thickly.

When Source chewed the banana, his nose bumped her clit.

"Fuck the fruit," he said.

❖ ❖ ❖

Scouts

Marsh is Source's best buddy, they used to play together in Scouts. Marsh visits their new apartment to drink beer and smoke dope. Nemah crawls into bed, waiting for the boys to spread the sleeping bag in the living room where Marsh will sleep.

"Wanna fuck Marsh?" Source whispers, snuggling in chilly beside her. Smells of beer and grass.

"No," she says, "only you."

He rubs her with his rough finger and she is getting wet. Wet. Bed creaks, blanket is lifted, Marsh pokes in beside Nemah. Source on one side, Marsh on the other, a sandwich with Nemah in the middle. Nemah is the meat. Boys are the bread.

"No," she says, pleading. She will pay for this. Later.

Source grabs her hand, the one touching him, and pushes it onto Marsh.

"Feel," he orders.

Strange. No foreskin, not like Source. She rubs the way she does with Source, up and down, around. Source kicks back the blanket and rises above her. Proud and erect like some god.

"Watch," he orders Marsh as he sinks inside her cream.

Nemah is growing cold. Cold as the blank winter sky hugging the streetlamp through the blue window glass, cold as the silver frost clinging to the pane of their prison. She tugs the blanket to cover them but Source kicks back impatiently.

"Watch," he says again. "I promised he could watch," he hisses at Nemah.

So Marsh watches, touching himself and barely breathing, as Source shows their private, private dance. When it is done, he creeps out silently, stealthy as a thief.

In the morning he is gone, the sleeping bag rolled up boy-scout tight and neat and cornered.

✣ ✣ ✣

Like sin

Bitterness hits Nemah at the back of the throat and in the gut like a fist. Like guilt. With Source, everything happens with the swiftness of a fist, bitter in the gut and throat. Like sin.

"You wanted to fuck Marsh," he screams, fists balled and ready.

Nemah cowers, whimpers, pleads. He will hit her anyway.

"I did not," she whispers.

It can make no difference. Source is not adjusted to reason. Perhaps this is something which she has chosen for herself. A thing she asks for. Source crying, Source weeping and Nemah is just cold, getting colder. No defence will make her right.

"Who else?" he screams. "I'll find out, you know I will. You might as well just say."

Dig my own grave. Write my own epitaph.

She is crunched tightly back against the wall.

"No one," she says. "Just me and you, that's all."

Fist slams the wall.

"Expect me to believe that?" he asks through his teeth.

Nemah winces, crumples.

"What about you?" she shivers.

Crazy crazy girl. Toss in that first shovelful of dirt, bury myself good. Seal it up tight.

Lithe as a panther, he lunges. Her neck under his hand. Now she is speechless. That'll teach her to shut up, slut.

Past erased, this is the real now. This is the only reality. These are the wages of my sin.

✣ ✣ ✣

I said he could

"I said he could fuck you," said Source. "I gave my permission."

"You can't do that," Nemah said. "You can't just give him permission."

Source sighed. "I can," he said patiently.

"What about me?" she asked. "You'll punish me."

"I'm not quite sure about that yet," he said.

"It wouldn't be fair," said Nemah. "I get beat and he has beers with you."

❖ ❖ ❖

Women bleed

Women bleed all over each other, spill their insides all over, which they call doing lunch, coffee—euphemisms for bleeding, expecting you to understand. Nemah never understands.

She goes with women to bars, someone to make certain she gets home if she doesn't pick up some guy. Someone to crawl around to find her where she has passed out. Someone to know whether or not she is alive in there, someone to watch over her.

Some say time for women is round but Nemah's time is straight ahead, straight behind. What is done is finished, she closes the door. So she thinks.

One night, Nemah and Anna-the-Witch do mescaline. Nemah is curious. Wonders what a woman might do. Source will kill her if he finds out and kill Witch too. Satisfaction comes from knowing she can have what Source cannot.

"You've wanted me all along," purrs Witch. "I knew it the moment we met."

"Yeah," hums Nemah, "ahhhh."

She can play women's games.

✣ ✣ ✣

Source drags

Source drags her by the hair across the church yard pavement while she screams for help. The Christian Youth Group, let out fresh and shiny from prayer meeting, stands by gawking. Their prayers have given no answers for this.

Leader Christian approaches Source.

"Should you be doing that?" he asks gently.

"Mind your own fucking business," Source barks. "This is none of your business."

Source jerks her to her feet. She feels her cheeks scraped and bleeding but no tears.

"This is mine," he tells Christian. "Mine!"

Christian backs off cowed and the little Christians scatter like chaff.

"You got your fucking audience. Are you satisfied now?"

Sure thing, she thinks, fine.

He never finds out about that Witch-thing.

❖ ❖ ❖

she makes him so

Source says he can't stop himself. There are moments when he is loving and Nemah sees that he is right but sees too that she cannot help him find that thing which he has not got. She feels his sadness, being trapped inside his anger as he is. He wishes he could stop, he says. It's just, he says, she makes him so mad.

Source cries. She used to make her dad so mad, too, only he never cried, just hit until he stopped. Until she cried. She has taught herself not to cry. Why can they not teach themselves not to hurt?

✣ ✣ ✣

panic hits

In the city bus panic hits like a boxer, Nemah pulls frantically at the cord, seems a lifetime till the bus stops. She gets up and out of there, she cannot look at anything, she cannot see. Feels like her heart will leap out of her throat, sees it bloodless, beating on the sidewalk.

I will stay in this bus, I will not try to escape. I am safe here.

Sometimes this talking to herself firmly works, but usually panic wins, she loses.

At the roadside, somewhere strange, Nemah gets lost. Has no idea. Nothing is real.

I am underneath a glass jar, underwater.

People walking by look glassy too. There is plastic film around them like a stretchy wrap. Their voices are hollow, tubed. She is stoned on angel dust with the world around her wrapped and warped.

The beating of her heart thumps her body, Nemah shakes and cannot stop.

In the checkout line or in the bus or in some elevator.

Nemah uses stairs, stays at home when fear is high in her.

"I feel like I'm underwater," she tells the doctor.

"What do you mean?" he asks.

"I can't say it any better," she says. "You are underwater, too, but separate from me. I have trouble hearing."

"Can you hear me now?" The doctor leans forward in his chair, hands thrust towards her.

Nemah shrinks back quickly and away. Shakes her head.

"Don't do that," she says. "It makes the dust appear."

The doctor settles back.

His lips move.

Nemah stares at them.

✣ ✣ ✣

Say sorry

One by one the children enter their mother's chamber.

"What am I supposed to say?" Nemah asks. She needs to understand the rules for this ritual, it is new to her.

"Say sorry," Sister whispers back.

"For what?" asks Nemah desperately.

"Everything. For whatever bad you did. Say, 'sorry for whatever bad I did to you Mommy.' Say, 'I love you Mommy.' "

From biggest to smallest, the children line up, say sorry, say love. When her turn arrives, Nemah approaches the big bed timidly, afraid. The lady is all in white, even her face. She stretches a pale, weak hand.

Tears have sprung to Nemah's eyes, she does not know why.

"Sorry Mommy," she whispers.

The white mouth opens, shuts, words come through a vacuum, Nemah cannot hear.

"For whatever bad I done," she whimpers. "Please Mama, don't die. I will be so very perfect, I will be whatever you want. Don't die. Don't."

A white hand falls listlessly to the handmade carded-wool blanket. Nemah tiptoes backwards as the tired eyes shut, dismissing. Closes the bedroom door stealthily. Breathes.

The house stays quiet as a tomb the rest of that day.

⁘ ⁘ ⁘

Brother tugs

Brother tugs down his fly in front of her face where she is reading.

"You wanna touch this?" he asks.

◆ ◆ ◆

martyr

Mother-wife-woman is martyr. Long-suffering and generous, she keeps husband-children-house all neat, carefully in their places. Tends to aging parents, keeps her place.

Inside the house and tucked away is the mother Nemah sees. Mostly she is hard as rock and black as anger. Nemah tries to tiptoe her way around her.

She is learning to shut up, be quiet, and to listen.

This is her knowledge: child obey your elders.

✣ ✣ ✣

hiding

Nemah hid behind the raspberry bushes in the garden she loved. The leaves smelled dusky. The crumbly red river dirt on which she crouched stuck to her knees in clumps.

She would always remember this hiding.

❖ ❖ ❖

the woman wept

Mother hid, too, behind her closed bedroom door.

Nemah was sad for her. She was helpless.

Behind the door, the woman wept.

When she talked, she said she never would have married if she had known.

"Known what?" Nemah asked her desperately.

"To have a husband, to have children," her mother said tiredly.

"Even me, Mama?" asked little Nemah, trying to cuddle in close.

"Never," said her mother.

So Nemah moved back and far away.

When her mother cried behind her shut door, Nemah knew it was her own sin that caused her mother's tears.

✣ ✣ ✣

that rope

"Who put that rope around your neck?" asks the doctor.

"I don't know, there is no face. She comes at night, ties me up and leaves me there alone."

"Can you see the face now?" he asks.

"Shut it out," Nemah says. She tugs hard. "There," she says with triumph and shoves her fistful of broken hair at the doctor. "For you," she says. "Something you can really see, something to believe in. Ropes and closets, those are for you to see or not. I want to make it go now."

"Including that swing and the happiness of the sandbox and the deep blue sky?" he asks.

Nemah tosses her hair gift on his desk.

"Even that," she answers. "Even that beautiful sky is filled with nothing more than anger. Even that happy sky is full of blood-lined clouds. Shut it out now."

✣ ✣ ✣

dismissed

"Could you have imagined it?" asks the doctor gently.

Nemah swallows heavily and tugs at her ragged scrub-brush hair. Loses her voice, cannot speak.

Trapped inside that darkened envelope, gleaming bars and wordless.

"Something you saw, perhaps, that worked itself into your subconscious mind," he says.

Her knuckles whiten and she tugs roughly at the hair. Satisfied, roots released, the pressure she feels is at least something. Something more than numb.

She lowers the handful of hair to her face for evidence and grins.

"Anything's possible," she says at last. "I suppose so. Something I saw maybe worked its way into my subconscious mind and now I think it really happened."

Raises her hand to the hair and tugs again.

"Shall I keep taking the stelazine?" she asks.

The stelazine means he believes she is psychotic. He would not tell her, so she looked it up for herself.

"And the Serax," he answers. "I'll see you tomorrow."

She is dismissed.

✣ ✣ ✣

Same old song

It's in your head, all in your head, you made it up, it never happened. Same old song, same old verse, same old tired tune.

YOU. WILL. OBEY. ME. CHILD.

Father rotten father whip in hand rotten to the mean core. Words lash meaningless, strike the air, fall down dead at Nemah's feet.

She steps on them, kicks them aside. Clods is all they are. Cleans them off her soles, disdains them. When she is mute, they cannot harm her.

The anger builds inside. She keeps it there, swallows it, buries it. It rots there, rots into her belly, leaves a rotten core. Sometimes she can taste it, that's how much rotten anger she holds inside.

She crucifies him in her mind. In her mind he hangs crucified but still undaunted, undiminished.

YOU. WILL. OBEY. ME. CHILD.

✣ ✣ ✣

Shut out

Shut out, shut out, shut everything out.

Man-the-father, woman-mother, those night-sights, shut them out. There will be no voice, no thought, no feeling when you disappear.

Nemah dances the fine line that separates raw reality from its twin.

We cannot hide from our dead forever.

Shut out, shut out, shut it all out.

Time passes and Nemah watches the life she has had dribble and flush itself away. Since the boxes can no longer keep her secrets, her crazy life is all around her and within her, crazy.

Shut out shut out shut it all out.

This singing dervish whirls inside her, she cannot force it to stop.

❖ ❖ ❖

The fetus grew

The fetus grew inside her like a cancer, she could not make it stop. In the morning she was sick, sick to her stomach, sick as sin. Fifteen years old, she had learned a lot. Just she did not know what to do about it. She knew where it had come from, she did not know how to make it go away.

Finally in August she saw a doctor. The doctor put his fingers inside her there where the baby was growing, he twisted them around. They hurt. He slid the paper sheet back around her belly, made her decent again. He told her mother she was pregnant.

"What do you want to do about this?" the doctor asked the mother.

Mother sat in the chair beside Nemah across the desk from the man with the plastic face.

"Make it go away," said Nemah, "that's what I want. Stop it."

The doctor talked to the mother, Nemah was invisible.

He told her mother how it could be done.

Mother twisted her capable, knotted fingers together on her lap. Her hands patted against the leather purse also on her lap.

The mother is the enemy. The plastic doctor could not know. Together, the strangers decided on a plan.

✣ ✣ ✣

seven in the morning

It is seven in the morning, dawn paints the prairie sky. The car is moving towards the dawn. East. Nemah is lying on blankets in the back like on some strange vacation. They are heading east.

She pukes into the plastic ice cream pail her mother has set on the floor by her head. The car makes her sick, this growing baby makes her sick.

Behind her mother's car is Source, driving with them but not with them. He is the guard. Make sure this thing gets done right. Nemah thinks of a funeral procession, all of them driving east towards the sunrise. She lies in back like a corpse laid out.

Mother signs her into the hospital, gives her consent to them knocking Nemah out, knocking out this tumour.

Someone comes, takes her away.

Behind her mother's anxious, angry face she sees Source. He smokes, he paces. Nemah wonders if they will sit together, if they will talk about her.

It is like any other surgery, they do the regular things, prepare her for anaesthetic. Nemah has done this part before. No one tells her anything, either you know it or you don't.

"You're pretty young for this," says the frigid nurse. "You shouldn't be here, you know."

"Count backwards from one hundred," says someone.

"Why one hundred?" she asks. When she is scared, she tries to laugh. She is crazy scared right now.

"Wake up, wake up."

Nemah tries to open her eyes, they are heavy as cement, as mountains. She feels, she hurts.

All I want is to sleep. To sleep and never open these gritty eyes, this sandpaper mouth.

"You have to wake up, it's time to go to the bathroom now."

The nurse drags Nemah up, she totes her to the washroom. Shoves her in, locks the door.

"When you're done, pull the cord," she says.

Nemah sits on the toilet. She is bleeding. She is bleeding more than ever before, she can't remember this kind of blood. Where is it all coming from? There is no baby, only this cancer that washes out from her private spot between her legs, spills into the white toilet beneath her.

Black spots swim inside her head.

In the car again, Nemah wraps the blanket tightly around her shoulders, wedges it roughly between her legs where all that blood is spilling out. Their procession home is led by Source. They have finished their funeral, the fetus is dead.

Nemah lies quiet in her blanket coffin and breathes. In. Out.

✣ ✣ ✣

everything changes

After the dead baby, everything changes. The beatings start.

Source gets power. Takes control.

Nemah drinks to get drunk and then she doesn't care anymore, the pain stops.

Pain no more.

✣ ✣ ✣

some deserted strip

Source parks the truck on some deserted strip road off the Trans-Canada. Leans across the seat, grabs her wrist. With his free hand, he shoves a tape into the player and cranks up the volume.

YOU'RE LAZY JUST STAY IN BED LAY-ZEE, it screams. LAY-ZEE LAY-ZEEE.

"This is for you," he taunts. "This is what you are. You'll never do anything. You'll never be any more than what you are right now."

Nemah whimpers, huddles miserably against the wall of accusation and sound while Source twists at her and tells her how she will never amount to anything.

"Why do you love me then?" she asks. "If I'm so fucking useless, why don't you just let me go?"

❖ ❖ ❖

good girl

"Have you been a good girl?" asks Source.

"Yes," Nemah says.

"Daddy's good little girl?" he asks, prodding.

"Good," she says, arching a little.

He pulls back. "Do you want me now?" he teases.

"Now," she sighs.

"Then say, 'I am Daddy's good little girl,' " he says.

"I'm Daddy's good little girl," she repeats.

"Say, 'fuck me please Daddy,' " he says.

"Fuck. Me. Please. Daddy," says Nemah succinctly through clenched teeth.

Source sinks into her sharply. She is wet and waiting.

✣ ✣ ✣

the last time

It has come to the last time that Source will beat her. Nemah has decided to leave. All her hidden plans are made, she has a bus ticket to Toronto. She will be swallowed by that city, gone.

This is the last time. The. Last. Time.

"My baby," he screams into her face.

He will kill her or he won't. Either way, she is out of it.

There was no baby, only fear. Only all that blood.

His veins stick out dark red, perhaps he will explode.

"I'm sorry," she says.

And means exactly that.

✣ ✣ ✣

bus trip on acid

This bus trip on acid, leaving Manitoba and hitting the United States border, Nemah was peaking. Mouth dry as lemon, she sucked back Cokes as the miles cracked by. Bus wheels droned constant against asphalt.

This get-away, an escape. Her exodus.

Source always said he could find her in hell.

"No matter where you go, I'll get you," he had promised. "I'll find you in hell if I have to."

She had thought hell was there with him.

"You wouldn't have very far to go then," she had said, as she laughed and ducked before his fist smashed. She had been reckless by then, with nothing much more or less to lose.

The acid was a going-away-good-luck gift from Lana.

"Do it after you get outta the city," Lana had made her promise. "Outta this hell-hole. Away from that shit-heel. Promise me."

Bus wheels drummed unchanging on the asphalt beneath the seat where she had found refuge and salvation colours.

Crossing the prairie border between countries, Nemah swallowed her Coke hard, ducked down in her seat but no one noticed. She could be invisible. Pushed her shades higher up the bridge of her nose and sniffled.

She leaned her cheek against the cold pane. Outside night had fallen, stars dotting the sky like candles, a million birthdays. Her eyes felt full and glassy but not from tears. Not from crying. This was her victory ride, she would not cry. She would feel those acid-colours wash over her, she would be a drift of wood.

He'll find me in hell if he has to.

But then that fullness behind her eyes melted down into sudden tears. Tears that drummed down her cheeks in rhythm with the wheels beating on the asphalt beneath her sanctuary.

"I am a one-note orchestra," she whispered like a mantra through those rusty tears.

Toronto Meats

Toronto Meats. Toronto Meats. Toronto Meats.

All the endless lonely night long the sign blinks neon onto Nemah's window.

Toronto Meats. Toronto Meats. Toronto Meats.

Under this winking neon are hung racks of bones. Goat bones. With heads attached. Skin-covered. Nemah watches the racks of dead goats dangle under the winking neon. Mouths agape and dead. She is sure of it. Dead.

Neatly bereft of fur, they seem only naked, and in their nakedness and deadness they seem obscene.

The cockroaches in her apartment obscene in their swift aliveness, the goats under winking neon, dead.

Being night-keeper has no logic here in this place, she is completely alone here. No monsters emerge from any closet, only endless cockroaches and dead, naked goats under flashing neon.

Nemah sits alone in the single creaky armchair all night watching out the window, for there is no life inside her one-room apartment. Sucks back valium like peppermint candy. Rewarding herself for every hour of her keeper duty.

Nemah ground her cigarette into the pearled shell on the doctor's desk.

"He's dead," she said sternly.

"Why do you believe that?" asked the doctor.

He raised his one quirky eyebrow briefly, then dropped it. The mask slid back down over his real face. Nemah blinked. She readjusted her sight to match his mask.

"This stelazine is making me feel weird," she said.

"Weird? How?"

"Funny. Not real. Kind of," she said.

"Unreal in what way?" he persisted.

Nemah dropped her hand from the butt in the shell. Traces of its form lingered on the desk. She lifted it like a dead weight from her lap and let it drop again. The traces moved from the desktop to the blank space where she had lifted it. She could sense its dead weight on her lap. Nemah blinked.

"My eyes feel sharp," she explained. "Sharp and wet. Like crystal. Sometimes I can't shut them."

She placed her dead hand against the nape of her neck.

"My neck gets stiff. All of a sudden. And I get paralyzed, petrified, I can't move."

"Why are you afraid?" the doctor asked.

"I can't write," said Nemah. "I feel stoned."

"Do you want to write?" he asked.

"Well yeah," she said. "Sort of. At least a letter or something. At least in my diary. I want to stop taking them."

"And do what."

"Feel normal. Feel," she said.

"What makes you believe he's dead?"

"Maybe I just wished it. Maybe that, do you think so?"

"Maybe."

Toronto Meats. Toronto Meats. Toronto Meats.

Hanging there under winking neon, neatly and obscenely dead naked. Source twists gently from the steel meat hook, gently twists, seductive in this morbid waltz, mouth agape. Hung by his feet with the hairless and the dead. The blood draining slowly from his open mouth into the stainless pail below.

Nemah sits in the armchair by her window in that tightly airless apartment as cockroaches dance around her feet. Radio crackles off-station, darkened envelope enwombs her. Watching the dead naked Source gently twisting the night away.

✣ ✣ ✣

No voices told her

After she had put enough inside her mouth and veins, no angels sang. No voices told her she was damned. No mother-father-beating, she could even forget about Source.

Nemah travelled light. It made it easier to get away when things got bitter.

✣ ✣ ✣

trapped in the penthouse

His foot stench permeates the penthouse suite. His feet must be rotted clear through, she is afraid to look at them. He never removes his socks.

He picked her up in the café across from the bus depot, now he has her trapped in the penthouse suite of the Holiday Inn overlooking the fountains of city hall.

He never takes off those socks but stalks the penthouse naked as a jaybird. In socks. Those feet would look like well-aged cheddar, all white and crumbly, or like feta.

She has thirteen cents, not enough for a subway token. Trapped in the penthouse. He borrowed the last of her money and does not repay her. Says he is from Buffalo. Says he imports cocaine. Orders room service and dines out and charges everything. Introduces her down the strip as his old lady.

She fucks him twice, like a handshake.

He gets off on something else, something else that Nemah does not understand. She fucks him because she thinks he expects it, then sees he doesn't.

❖ ❖ ❖

In Toronto she lived

In Toronto she lived with Guy, he played rhythm guitar in a band, they wanted to be famous.

He wandered off for days, then reappeared without a sound.

Nemah went with Guy to score, he left her there with Base and went to get some money for the peyote.

Nemah sat on Base's bed, she counted buttons in her head.

The Joy of Sex was there, she flipped through it, wasting time till Guy came back.

"Do some," said Base. "You can pay me later."

He set four buttons on the open page of couples screwing, left the room.

She ate one, then one more. She left the other two.

"Pay me now," he said.

Obediently she spread her legs.

✣ ✣ ✣

some albino biker

She fucked some albino biker in their clubhouse.
Others came to share the spoils.
Then she went back home.
Guy never noticed she had been gone.

❖ ❖ ❖

Turn over

"Turn over," he ordered.

She turned, face to the window, felt him stiffen against her spine, then lower. Inside.

"Shit," he said, reached for the K-Y handy at his bedside. Tore into her.

Passive, she lay accepting this humiliation.

Boys, that's what he really wanted. Some boy.

✥ ✥ ✥

A nice girl like you

"A nice girl like you in a place like this. Why do you do such things, a nice girl like you."

"Come, sit on my face, baby."

"Commere blondie, hey blondie, sit on my lap, we'll talk about the first thing that pops up, hah hah."

"Whaz th' matta cooty, cummere."

One by one she jerks them off, the fat men and the thin.

Cum on her hands, her chin, she doesn't notice.

It does not matter, makes no difference at all.

Bits of baby, all that sperm.

Nemah is good at this job. They ask for her by name.

"Blondie," they say.

❖ ❖ ❖

some sort of mark

Nemah fucks the drummer once, at her apartment. The next morning she throws him out.

By five o'clock, four of his friends have called on her.

She checks the outside of her door for some sort of mark. Nothing visible.

The next one who calls comes in. It costs him thirty and a reefer.

Nemah thinks she let him off for cheap.

✣ ✣ ✣

touched him, she hurt

Schizophrenic Jak, Nemah touched him, she hurt. She never knew who he would be, she loved him all.

She thawed into his dancing hands, let him suck her nipples no matter who he was. He rolled over, melted into her. Grew inside her fist as hard as mountain, soft as moonshine. With Jak she came and came and came.

Outside the sky turned pink over garbage cans, the Don Valley glistened in the sunrise.

Cockroaches danced.

Nemah sang.

✣ ✣ ✣

just this time

Jak delivered her a poem, "Hail Beauty Full Clown of Sorrow."

To the poem he attached a self-portrait of Vincent van Gogh, the one with the big bandage over the place where his ear had been.

He cut it off himself to get rid of the pain, said Jak, then painted himself a portrait.

Together they pored over the book.

Nemah read the present, she had no words.

Jak lifted his guitar and played and there was nothing else, no more than that.

Just the time, just this time.

❖ ❖ ❖

Jak rolled over

While Jak was away in California, he dreamed a dream, drew it, and mailed it to Nemah.

He wrote he was rooming with an old rich fag, he said the fag left him alone, said he was a whore for his art.

Nemah fucked the drummer again while Jak stayed rent-free on the coast.

I will not sit here alone and wait, she thought, no strings, no strings.

When Jak came back, he was empty.

Nemah held him close, he turned away. Cradled against his back, she pressed him into her palm, felt him grow. She wrapped herself around him.

She would have done anything, anything in the world.

Jak rolled over, pushed away her hand.

Pressed himself into himself, stroked himself and he was soothed. Loved himself until he came. Grunted. Fell asleep.

Nemah tossed a towel beside him to fill the space where she had been. He twitched and muttered.

She pulled on her jeans, roamed the streets till dawn.

The boys in the band were home, Nemah went in for the party.

❖ ❖ ❖

easy money

Nemah watches these naked men forming their own excitement. Touching each other and she is paid to watch. Just to watch, it is easy money.

But in her stomach, a lump builds, a hard knot.

These men are foolish, among them there is too much wasted flesh.

Women waste no flesh, Nemah thinks. They use it all.

✣ ✣ ✣

Isobel weakens

She goes down on Isobel when Isobel has her period. Spreads those sulky lips, laps quickly, sucking in Isobel's blood. Sucks it in raw.

"No," Isobel says, turns her head sideways and refuses to meet Nemah's eyes. Shuts tight her knees and locks herself up, away from Nemah's eager mouth.

"Please," begs Nemah. "Just a taste, please." She is greedy now with lust, refusing to take the "No" Isobel has given. "I'll bet you let Jobe."

Isobel weakens, unlocks her thighs. She likes the jealousy.

Nemah lowers her head, tongue tingling. Isobel pants while Nemah sucks her blood.

"Nobody ever did that to me before," she says and Nemah laughs while Isobel comes.

"I don't think it's normal," Isobel says later when she is curled against Nemah's belly like some kitten.

Nemah giggles.

"Just as normal as anything," she says.

✣ ✣ ✣

scratches

Nemah scratches Isobel's skin raw and then licks at the red threads that appear. She is craving the taste of Isobel-blood.

Isobel tends Nemah's wounds where Source has touched her. Where bruises grow, both visible and not.

Nemah hides Isobel from Source and then, after Source, Isobel has no more of herself to share. She dries up the love, it withers and dies. Nemah is bereft.

Source was the glue that bound them together.

⁘ ⁘ ⁘

Carla the landlady

Carla the landlady of the rooming house by the Don Valley turned dealer when her child left for school in the morning. By three-thirty she was the mother again.

Pay the money, Carla fixes for the day, the week, depends how much you score. Stretch out your arm, she prods the vein. Swallow hot saliva quick, the point sinking through flesh meeting the blood hot and sweet. This rush tastes like sex. You come when Carla does you. She takes your money first. Carla doesn't mess around. She's clean, her veins are clean.

Once Nemah reaches for Carla, but that moment passes and then is gone. It was Isobel she wanted anyway, it was the blood on her tonsils that made her think of Isobel.

✣ ✣ ✣

the blood

"Why do you need the blood?" asked the doctor.

Nemah was silent, suddenly ashamed.

"I can't talk now," she said finally. "It's not something I tell about."

⁘ ⁘ ⁘

The lead cracked

"The pain only grows because you let it," said the doctor.

"So you keep telling me," snapped Nemah. "You and my mother, what a team."

He snapped the HB to his desk. The lead cracked.

She imagined blood leaking from his hand where he had clenched the pencil. Her mouth watered.

"I'm so sorry," she said.

⁘ ⁘ ⁘

did not die

Although not hell, Source found her in Toronto.
Smashed in her head, then left.
"Forget you ever knew me," he told her.
Nemah did not die.
He had lost his power.

✣ ✣ ✣

easy words

"You have to forgive yourself first," said the doctor. He nestled the HB in the stiff copper spirals of his beard. "It's not your fault, you did not deserve any of it. If you stop hurting yourself, the pain will stop."

Nemah rubbed her dry palm against the scaley bald patches on her scalp where she had been pulling out her hair.

"You can say that," she said. "It's all just easy words to you. A prescription, a cure. There is no cure to this. It only grows and builds."

"It grows and builds until you disarm it," he said.

She watched him braid coppery spirals of beard around the yellow HB in his capable hand. She watched the curls spring back into place.

"Maybe my hair will come back in curly like your beard," she said. "Curly and rusty like some old nail."

✣ ✣ ✣

bruises

Blood caked crusty, mouth tight and cracked, bruises spotted across bare white breast and shoulder, her belly glistens with cold slick semen. Nemah sinks down beside the clawfoot tub, caresses the floor. There is no logic. Someone invited here has done this to her and has left. Has left no clues. Only this. This damage and no memory of it.

Nemah cannot stop shaking.

✣ ✣ ✣

no sad songs

There are no sad songs. There are none sadder.

She doesn't want to hear them anymore.

She closes her heart, shuts her soul.

Sing me no more sad songs, she tells herself. Sing me no more.

✣ ✣ ✣

In the nuthouse

In the nuthouse, there is another like her. Evenings they get passes to leave the hospital because no one believes they are really sick at all, just pampered spoiled babies wanting attention. If they leave the hospital, they are considered healthier. Or at least on the road to recovery. Nemah does not want to leave the hospital, where she is secure. Where there is no booze. But eventually she gets stir-crazy.

Staff watch her go into the bathroom and come out. They won't let her take in her razor to shave her legs even though she is not considered suicidal.

She must ask permission to have her toothbrush. She begs for her razor. Staff suggest she could shave in her room with the door open. Fortunately she has a room to herself, they are short of crazy people, it must be a late winter lull. The ones they do have, though, more than make up for the ones they lack.

An old man in a wheelchair has to be fed his pablum like some tiny helpless newborn. He spits up, they scoop it all neatly back onto the spoon and pop it back inside his o-mouth, scolding all the while.

"Now, now, Mr. Fuchs, eat like a good boy," they cajole.

They have given him enough shock treatments to light up all of Winnipeg for twenty years. Just in case he might want to come to more often than once a week, just to be on the safe side.

Every once in a while old Mr. Fuchs comes to long enough to demand a cigarette and from time to time his wrinkled hand pushes down his zipper and begins to masturbate that soggy penis vigorously. When that happens, Nemah watches through lidded eyes the staff scold and whack the child-claw away from self.

"Naughty, naughty Mr. Fuchs. Mustn't touch, mustn't

touch."

They zip him back up respectable as quick as quick.

He stares bewildered. Demands a cigarette.

"Tseegarret," he howls. "Tseegarret!"

Staff scamper to fill his desire. Let him kill himself. Let him take the rap himself.

There are endless crosswords to do to occupy her time. Aside from the entertainment of old Mr. Fuchs there is little else. Staff arranges afternoon bingos. Those who can walk are trying to walk somewhere. To Japan. Every morning they don coats, scarves, boots, mittens and walk together to the Golf Course Coffee Shop on the outskirts of the town.

First they are given their medications. Half an hour ahead to make sure they take effect. Those who are med-changes, stabilizations, shock-ready, those simply too loony to leave the grounds, are kept back.

All the rest have to go, there is no choice. Nemah does not respond well when she has no choice, but there it is. Sometimes she can pretend she is escaping. The walk there and back has been methodically clocked and when they return to the hospital they add their mileage to a chart on the wall. Chances are no one there now will ever see the results of their clocking. If they ever make it to Japan. And if they do, what will happen then? Will they stay for tea? Will they walk back to Canada? Will they be allowed to stay in Japan?

When they arrive at the coffee shop they enter as a group, sit, and have coffee. They smoke cigarettes. Flirt with each other and the waitresses. Nemah wonders whether the waitresses know they are from the nuthouse. She wonders whether they are frightened. Wonders if their fingers are poised on cop shop redial.

✣ ✣ ✣

Old Johann

Old Johann is perhaps thirty-five, he is cute for old and Nemah likes him. His soft brown eyes grow misty when he talks about his wife and kids, he must miss them a lot, he must love them very much.

In the coffee shop, Nemah listens to Myrna talk, filling up her ears with nuthouse gossip.

Old Johann burnt up his kids in the barn, Myrna says. The day before, she says, he poured gasoline all around, on the hay and in the haystack, all around the outside and inside walls, to prepare. Then, the next day, he told his kids to go into the barn, wait for him.

He used to beat them all the time, she says, so when he gave an order, they listened. They listened and did just what he said.

So there they were, the five- and four-year-old and the twins who were seven, waiting for Daddy. Then he bolted that barn door from the outside, lit up a smoke and tossed it against the side of the barn. The whole thing just went up like a bonfire.

Old Johann just stood there, watching. Listening to the kids scream. He just stood there. And he smelled that stink.

If you singe your hair when you light a smoke take a good whiff, kids. Imagine kids, bodies burning.

Stood there and smelled that smell and listened and maybe heard.

Old Johann, what a sweetie, what a sensitive guy, what a lover. Said he was insane, says God made him to do it, sacrifice those kids. God told him to do stuff he didn't want to do. God made him stand there and smell that stink of burnt alive.

They put him in here. Not jail, just the nuthouse. Shock the shit out of him, shock the God out of him.

Nemah hears Myrna, she takes this story and tucks it away inside her brain where it will be safe. Sometime she may take it out and look at it but this is not the time. This is time for her. For herself. Johann flirts with her when he is between shock-times.

She adds too much sugar to her coffee, she cannot swallow, her throat refuses to swallow that syrup. She walks back against biting wind to the nuthouse. Towards Japan. Tea-time. She walks quickly, ahead of the rest. She inhales great breaths of prairie wind. She will make it back before anyone. She will take them all single-footedly to Japan.

❖ ❖ ❖

red roses to the nuthouse

There is no place else to go to dry out, no one to say you're not crazy, just a drunk. Just a drunk. When the system gets ahold of you it makes you one of those crazy ones, the ones the system knows. It assumes the booze is only a symptom of deeper problems. Nemah thinks she has no deeper problems.

Fortunately there are drugs for insanity.

These symptoms of insanity can be controlled. Patterns can be changed by the filling of a syringe. Or the infusion of electricity. Power-pak. Recharge. Talk is another control, they call it therapy. You tell your darkest secrets and they use them against you, call it therapy.

Graham and Nemah mix their stabilizing meds with booze. They find small pubs around the nuthouse and visit in their pass-time. Their doctors think they are getting too serious about one another, they think there is a relationship developing between them.

This relationship is about the marriage of booze and pills.

On this side and that side there are pleasures, there are pains. Somewhere in the middle is where Nemah is expected to sit. Sit on that fine line down the middle wherein space becomes raw.

On the weekend after Graham has been to see his daughter he brings Nemah red roses to the nuthouse. She presses the petals in her photo album and keeps them there long after they have become broken and brown. Tucks them in a box, carries it around with her.

✣ ✣ ✣

Those boxes

"Those boxes in my apartment have got to go," Nemah said. "They are holding the anger and the pain. They have to be gotten rid of."

"Can you take care of them yourself?" asked the doctor.

"Everyone is in them," she said. "Dead babies and Isobel."

"So they have to go," he said. "Can you do it?"

"With vodka," she said. "Valium. Heroin. Yeah, I can do it. With."

"By yourself?"

"I just said," Nemah answered impatiently, "they all have to be killed again. I can do it, but not like this. Not sober."

"We'll work on it," he said.

"I want them out. They've stolen enough from me."

"When you are ready," the doctor said. He settled the sharpened tip of the HB against the pointed tip of his WASP nose.

"My scalp is itchy," Nemah complained. "Where the hair is growing back. It's so fucking itchy."

✣ ✣ ✣

She heard fuck

She heard fuck on the school grounds.

When the girl who said it told her, Nemah said "No."

"The dad puts his pee-thing in the mommy's pee-thing, it makes a baby," said the girl.

"No," said Nemah, "my dad never. Not my mom."

"Yeah," said the girl. "Did too, you betcha. They got you kids, didn't they? It's the only way."

✣ ✣ ✣

the only one

When Nemah went to the bathroom she touched herself with her finger and felt a good twinge. Shivers felt good all over her, even inside her mouth. She peed hot pee onto her hand and watched her naked self in the mirror.

I must be the only one.

The only one who feels this stuff, the sickest one on earth.

✣ ✣ ✣

she throws a party

The parents leave and she throws a party. Not that she knows how. The three guys and Nemah's best girlfriend, they are all thirteen.

She plays Jim Morrison on the portable record player left by the brothers now in universities.

She lights candles and incense. The guys want to smoke. She gives them saucers, the old and chipped china used for camping. Opens the windows to let the smoke escape.

Shane is there, she wants him. He is gorgeous but really stupid, in the slow-learners' class while Nemah is smart.

"I wanna fuck with him," she tells Maria in whispers and they both giggle maniacally.

"Go upstairs," says Maria. "I'll tell him to go find you."

Nemah goes, she holds her breath in her bedroom, sitting on the green ruffled bedspread that matches the curtains that match the wallpaper.

Her heart beats wildly, she holds her breath. Licks her lips.

Through her little window the streetlight shimmers on glistening snow like diamonds.

Touches her mouth, wets her fingertip, rubs the saliva over her right eyebrow.

Downstairs there is wild laughter and the record stops playing. She waits and waits, the time is growing thin and stretched.

Nemah's back is to the door when she hears footsteps, perhaps not his. His hand on her shoulder, or perhaps not his. She hardly dares to turn around. Feels lips on her neck. His.

He pushes her on the bed, she can scarcely believe she is there with him.

Expects a kiss. His hand on her chest, her heart is beating fast.

"Let's fuck," he grunts and then his fingers are on her belt, her zipper, he tugs at the jeans she wore for him.

She pulls away, he moves too quickly, she expected more time.

"No," she says too late.

There is flesh, wobbly, sickish, between her thighs and on her belly.

"No," she says again.

She thinks she has a voice.

The cord stretches, then it snaps.

He grunts, her thighs get sticky, pulls up his jeans. She cannot look, it hurts to try to see.

"I got raped," she tells Maria later.

Maria giggles, laughs.

"You asked for it," she says.

✣ ✣ ✣

Why not spit

Why not spit it out for godsake, say let's fuck. It's easier than wading through the bullshit. But she won't help. Expects him to figure this one out on his own. If she says it, she'll be responsible. She knows his wife doesn't understand him, she's heard it all before. It's not that different.

"Let me tuck you in," Murphy says and nuzzles at her. Greedy.

He can't tuck her in, this is no bed and there is no bedding here. A euphemism, she knows. He is eager now, panting, breathing hard. She presses against his bulk and she is breathing too. She just doesn't want the euphemisms, doesn't need the bullshit.

Yeah, they could fuck. It would be like old times. She could do it this once. At least he won't move in, she won't have to pick up his socks or close the toilet after him. She won't have to be the mother again. Not this time; he has a wife already.

She bites his lips, his thick tongue, licks his nose, oh christ he does. Makes her hot despite the belly and the thick fur on his chest. Presses herself to his bulk, softening belly, and his hard. Yeah, she could compromise.

And then here he is, becoming familiar and then she can't stop, doesn't want to stop and this sudden fierce and angry jealousy hits her hard like a surprise.

Don't ask, don't tell, don't say. I don't really want to know, just want to fuck and fuck and feel this pleasure. Like Siamese twins with shared everything and there you are and here I am. I am, I am, I am.

"You still put your jeans on just the same," he says.

"A fluke," she says, "haven't put them on this way for years." And it's true.

While he lies back smug on her couch rubbing his belly, she hurries on her jeans. It's time for him to leave, leave now, but he just lies there. Looking.

"Was it good for you?"

I can't believe you said that. Can't, won't answer. Won't give that satisfaction. You can't have it all. Not this time. Not yet.

Instead, she laughs.

Don't ask.

Jeaned, she leans against him, proud bareness and new softness, toys with the dark hairs on his thigh, smells the rye she did not drink. It's on her breath, absorbed through her pores, she feels as drunk as Murphy says he is.

I'm dripping your juice. You didn't have to spill so much.

❖ ❖ ❖

early March

Walking with Murphy in early March, seems like spring but everyone says there is one more big one coming. Each beside the other. They passed the old apartment where once they played at love together and neither said anything about that. She couldn't tell if he was thinking, too, about that bed where once in play he pretended to tie her up and have his way with her.

They are old friends now.

They approach a bridge built only to carry a pipe across the river. She wants to cross but there is a twenty-foot gap between the end of the bridge and the riverbank. Just like her life.

Opening her cigarette case, she pulls out a reefer. Lights up. "No thanks," he says, "but you can."

There was a time when Murphy could have said it, given his permission, but that time has passed. She wants to take his hand, hold on, but that is no longer natural. Walking again, she slips the roach back into the pack and tugs at the jacket he had offered from his car. Does up the snaps and shivers.

Hands so cold. As ice. As death.

She wants to hold his hand. Shoves hers into her pockets.

In the car she asks if she can smoke. He has quit, she remembers.

"My wife smokes," he says, and she notices one long lipstick butt in the ashtray.

Relief. She isn't purely perfect. Wife.

Christ, I am so very cold.

Blows on her hands, curled, frozen, and he takes one, holds it as though it is his. It's warmer. It's warming and she pulls it back as though burnt.

✣ ✣ ✣

a settlement

"It was a settlement," Murphy tells her. "Nothing more, nothing less. It was the easy thing to do. I didn't even have to think about it."

Passes the reefer thin and potent, suck on that.

"The rest of the marriage isn't so bad. I can get by, make do. Not so bad."

Nemah tugs him into her mouth, twists her angry tongue around that hard head.

"Easy?" she asks. "Like me? Like this?"

Suddenly, ferociously aware that someday she might be dismissed as easily. Lapping dew from that egocentric head under her tongue.

"Like me?"

Rubs her hand down hard and hears him groan. Disbelieving.

✣ ✣ ✣

On their anniversary

On their anniversary, Jonathan's mother treated them to dinner. Nemah choked on salad, coughed in the restroom with the sit-down mirrors and Kleenex dispensers built-in. There she puked, the lettuce and tomato.

Make room for wine, space for valium.

Counted yellow tablets, only five. At least there was wine.

Husband-stillness, she was frozen out.

This silence is killing me.

At home during the day she studied the wedding photographs, searching for some clue, some promise.

At night, she lay beside him, blank space between them. He kept himself away. Curled apart, he had no needs anymore that she could reach.

Nemah touched the hollow space inside herself and she lay barely breathing.

Face wet, fingers wet, she came beside him barely breathing.

Filled herself with herself while silence grew and then she cried. Caressed his back inside the night, he took her hand in sleep.

Rocked her back and forth in fetal fashion till he awoke.

✣ ✣ ✣

smoking

"I used to think I'd be a poet," Nemah said.

The doctor shifted in his chair, leaned back. Cigarette instead of pencil jabbed between his fingers, painted them bronze. He tapped it on the shell.

"Why did you start smoking again?" she asked. "I thought you gave it up."

"Can you write now?" he asked. Smoke echoed from his tongue.

"The pen is unfamiliar," she said. "It feels so small. I hold my poems in a box behind the door. My journals too."

"Those boxes hold a lot of pieces, don't they?" he asked.

"Just junk, I think," she said, fidgeting in her chair. She tapped her nails on the wood between them. "I also thought I'd be a singer or be a teacher, I thought I'd get some life out of this."

"Do you read them?" he asked.

"I try, the letters jiggle," she said. "I lost the focus for those things."

"What will you be now?" he asked. A freshly lit cigarette hovered against his beard.

"Nothing. There is no market for these talents I have now," she said. "I have become redundant."

"Are you still seeing that married guy?" he asked.

Nemah tapped her fingers, slowly built a steeple. Made it fall.

"He has this wife," she said. "He says she makes things easy, he likes it that way. Easy. Not like me who thinks too much, fucks too much."

"Are you done with him?" he asked.

"I think," she said. "Anyway, I need a woman now."

She tasted blood and swallowed fast.
The doctor punched his cigarette to death.

✤ ✤ ✤

you say you're busy

Sure, anyone can play that game. I call you up to tell you I'm moving and you say you're busy. Get back to you later, say you. We haven't talked in over two years and now you're busy. Oh Isobel, if that's the game, I wrote the fucking rules. Wow, was I ever drunk last night, old shit, we can play it now. But how can you, with me?

Your hands on me smooth as the river, soft as dawn, your breast your mouth your mouth lost in it your eyes.

She calls back. Five minutes later.

"Hello," says Nemah, all business, clipped and cool.

"Hi," says Isobel, cozy as a feather bed. "You still home?"

"Home," says Nemah and laughs because.

My palms get wet. I hear your voice, your breath, you stumble over your words trying to sound gay because you remember how a tone can send me spiralling down.

"Could I come?" asks Isobel, voice lilting, emphasis on come.

Sounds sweet like music, like singing, Isobel.

"You tell me," says Nemah and laughs again. Because.

"I'll bring the wine," says Isobel sweetly.

Was I drunk last night, was I ever.

"I think. When?"

"After ten. After work."

"What about Jobe? Are you still together?" asks Nemah.

"After ten," she repeats, ignoring.

"He's out of town, right?" *Stay out of it. That's hers, belonging to Isobel.* "There's boxes everywhere, I've packed the glasses."

"I'll bring glasses. We can drink from the bottle, we can do that. A paper sack if necessary. I want to see you. Need to, after all this time."

My hands slippery on the receiver, switch to the other ear. Don't say anything.

"What?" Nemah asks.

Say it again. Please.

"After ten," Isobel says.

Dial tone. She would not repeat it, not even once. Not even just one time. Later she might. Later, after half a bottle of wine maybe, and then, afterwards, it will be, "man was I ever drunk last night, was I ever."

After the wine, Nemah will ask about Jobe again.

"He doesn't understand my needs," she will say. *And she'll lick inside my ear where "needs" has landed. Oh Isobel.*

"My needs," she will say. "He's hard and he's angry and he hits me."

And oh shit what will I say then, what will I say?

Hits. You. Isobel of mocha eyes, cappuccino skin, liquid limbs and fluid touch.

Hits. You.

Hits.

He hits.

Jobe hits Isobel.

My Isobel.

Isobel brings the wine, the dry white wine, and they sip, Nemah from her open mouth.

Drink it, suck it in. Share the wine giggling amid my life stuffed in boxes all neatly stacked around.

✥ ✥ ✥

toilet

The toilet had flooded and kept spilling like some waterfall. Nemah tried not to think of it but there it was, every time she climbed the stairs. Like some demon-child, there it was at the top.

Isobel had come and gone. She would not be back.

Nemah stopped using that toilet and used the one in the basement instead. Eventually, she would have to leave the house. The sewage and that basement would evacuate her. She would be forced to give herself up. Meanwhile she lurked behind the windows guarded by glass, watching and waiting.

Mute. Frozen. Paralysis of the brain. Nothing worked anymore. It was all, all of it, oozing with sewage.

✣ ✣ ✣

hunters

Another round, another.

Kill this.

Nemah sucks it in until no voice talks inside her head.

"They've closed the bar, let's go," says Gloria-the-keeper.

Nemah is obedient, carries the glass, an ashtray, all the swizzle sticks she can gather. Proof she has been there. Proof she has been.

Stripper in the lobby has made-up features sketched meticulously over real ones in mask. Nemah stares hard at those crimson nipples drawn over real ones underneath. Then she understands. Looks away ashamed.

It gets her by. It is the hunters to be wary of, not the hunted.

⁂

this dry-out rehab

At this dry-out rehab they take away her pills. They take her shampoo, gel, shaver, and her toothpaste too.

"Why are you taking all my stuff?" she asks.

"Alcohol," says the woman. "You use it to get high."

"Shampoo?" she asks. "Toothpaste?"

"You alchies take the cake," the woman mutters. "All so fuckin' innocent."

"Do I get to wash my hair?" she asks.

"Wait here for Miz Braun," says the woman.

She leaves a trail of twisting snakes behind her where she walks.

Nemah watches those snakes coil themselves around each other on the floor. She raises her feet so they can't get at her. Clenches her hands around her knees on the chair.

"You must be Nemah," says the woman. Cheer is all over her face, she must be on bennies.

"Must be," says Nemah.

The woman sits poised, pen in hand, asks address, date of birth.

Nemah answers.

"How much do you drink a day?" she asks.

"Two bottles of wine, $2.59 a bottle," Nemah says. "Cheap Canadian."

The woman writes it down.

"What drugs?" she says.

"Stelazine and Serax, valium, Divol, he gave me Elavil for a while," says Nemah. "I've been on Vivol and Ativan, the Halcion for sleep at night. I gave them all to that woman who left the snakes."

"That's it?" she asks.

"I'm thinking fuzzy," Nemah says. "Haven't had my valium

today and no wine. I thought I'd get a head start, save some time."

"Are you sure about all this?"

"Pretty," says Nemah. "I'm sorry I'm so shaky, it's been this way today."

By the end of day one, Nemah is screaming inside.

Day two, she is out of her mind. Day three she starts convulsions. They put her back on stelazine, they give her Dilantin.

Dry-out is supposed to take three weeks. After four, Nemah is still sick. The rehab doctor with the slimy hands tells her that her liver is too healthy, she must be lying about the wine.

"Yes," she says. Anything.

He says she has an infected uterus, gives antibiotics, tells her no sex for ten days.

Nemah cannot even count her fingers. She agrees.

God, they talk about God. God sucks, she thinks inside her head twisted around in plastic wrap. *God is dead, fuck God, fuck God.*

She smiles and keeps to the back of their meeting room.

Sausages and bacon and pork chops. Nemah hides in the stairwell when the others eat. The smell, it makes her throw up.

Furtively she phones the doctor.

"I can't stand this," she shivers into the pay phone, hears him click his lighter.

"What can I do?" he asks at last.

"Give me back my pills," she begs. "I need them to survive. I'll cut out the booze, I promise. Just give me back my pills."

Doctor inhales. Exhales.

"I'm sorry it's so hard for you," he says. "I can't help you anymore. Come see me when you're out of there, okay?"

She stands there listening to the drone of nothing in the January frost.

✣ ✣ ✣

Dry-out hell

Dry-out hell. There's nothing worse than this.

✣ ✣ ✣

Divorce, he says

"Well-preserved," Jonathan calls her now.

Preserved. Like some fruit, some vegetable. Preserved in booze. All these years, kept frozen. Frozen body, brain, soul.

Divorce, he says.

Now he can afford it, now he is ready. Not when she asked, not then.

"It was a mistake," Jonathan says, "a mistake."

I am no one's mistake. Will not allow it.

"I thought I wouldn't be able to do this," he says.

"This." He means me.

"I'm so glad we could finally do this."

Perched like some great bird at the farthest edge of her couch, as far from her as he can be, holds his body like some precious commodity. Perhaps he thinks she might boldly reach out. Touch him. Holds himself so fragile. He has no way of knowing he has nothing to fear, she has lost the ability to touch, if she ever had it. She will not tell him now.

"My first love," he tells her. "First true love."

She watches his mouth curl around the phrase so tenderly, as though the words mean something more than the sounds she hears. She stores it, will piece together this puzzle later. Now is not the time. Now there is no time.

"Mistake," he repeats. "A mistake."

A chill of guilt forms. His life all clean and bare and careful. Except for her. Made your fucking point, it's been made.

"I was partly to blame," he says. "I was never really mad at you. Well maybe once but never really."

Here we go 'round the fucking mulberry bush. Bite your tongue. Be a good girl.

Jonathan's words have accomplished nothing.

He turns himself away, it doesn't surprise her.

"I need to hug you," she says.

He is stiff to the touch.

"What?" he asks. Turns.

She raises herself on tiptoes, he is still too tall for her.

"You're still too tall," she says.

"What?" he asks, "what?"

"Tall," she says. "Too tall."

Awkward, she fills the space between them with nonsense. The space is between them. When he leaves, the space between them is gone. It is inside her now. She tastes it on the back of her tongue, it tastes sad.

Closing the door behind him, locking it. Old doors are closing all around her.

✣ ✣ ✣

spoken all of it

Nemah thinks she has spoken all of it, there is nothing else inside. She has become a shell. There are no drugs anymore that she can take. This final drying-out has worked. Now she can get on with life.

"Real life sucks," she tells the doctor. "Sucks the bag."

She smoothes her hair, finally growing back in. It feels silken, childish.

"I feel like some kind of virgin," she says and smiles.

"Can you empty the boxes now?" he asks, and slides the ashtray across the desk at her.

Nemah's hand shakes, she lights the cigarette crisply.

"Perhaps I'll just move again," she says.

"What will happen to the boxes?" he insists.

Nemah breathes, watching the smoke form a tunnel from her mouth and nose.

"I suppose I'll have to give up smoking, too," she says. "Now that I'm clean. I've given up everything else, I may as well."

Exhales a smoke tunnel.

Smiles with her clean new mouth.

✣ ✣ ✣

camera

Nemah feels weighed down, the camera too heavy, the strap threatening to choke the life out of her.

"What do you think you will see?" asked the doctor.

"I will see through the lens what my eyes cannot."

She will shoot everything, she will shoot the town. The houses of Isobel and of Source. The camera may tell her the truth of these matters.

Trees slide by, coloured leaves crimson and copper, rust and golden, she aims at those colours more vivid than real.

"Will you take a taxi?" he asked.

"Walk," she said. "Everything there is in the same place."

Main Street. Shoots the post office, the cars, the old women in black with kerchiefs and enormous pockets. Their pursed lips, tightened eyes, anger lines.

Kids slouching, poised to run.

Isobel's street just off Main. No thinking, just recording. But the clear-swept lawn and single heavy oak catch at her, threaten to tug her in.

This is the home of Isobel's mother, she thinks. This is the home of mocha-skinned Isobel.

Record, aim, shoot.

Walks on heavily, she can nearly taste Isobel's sweet cum on her tongue. But not quite.

Down Isobel's street and around the corner where Source was suckled. Resting against a fence, she records the salmon-coloured stucco and the brown shuttered windows behind which Source was raised.

Next was hers, she did not need a compass. She could find that house blind.

There is no other path like the path home.

Nemah's feet carry her through the images of one thousand

nightmares. Her camera creates a shield between herself and that house.

She shoots the pictures she thinks she will need. As a dream, no more real than the images in her memory.

✣ ✣ ✣

lit the red candle

Nemah returned to her apartment alone.

She kicked angrily at the boxes stacked around the doorway.

Found matches in her bag and lit the red candle. Slumped to the floor, her back against the rigid radiator, and watched the flame dance with its reflection in the window glass.

The line along which she madly spun still stretched ahead.

⋄ ⋄ ⋄

hole-in-the-wall

Nemah sat in her apartment, the hole-in-the-wall downtown where rent was still cheaper.

"This is a drunk's apartment," she thought. "Some dive. This is not for me anymore."

The boxes lurked behind the door and in her closet.

What was inside the boxes kept her angry, chained her to the darkness. Filled with bitter words spilled over onto paper, those words reached out like accusing fingers to Nemah, keeping her in bondage wherever she happened to be. And those mementoes from when she was still trying to be so perfect, when she was young enough to believe she might still win. When the odds did not seem so steep.

Poems, journals, endless letters to herself.

Nemah was sober, still sober, it made her hurt all over. Worse than any punch or kick or twisted fingers. She was heavy as a rainforest, dry as dust inside.

Now that she held the weight of all those things inside up close to her edges, they were spilling out, there was no way to dam them up anymore. She remembered everything.

With heavy feet, Nemah dragged two of the crates to the middle of the floor. Sat cross-legged, yoga-like, with heavy feet.

✣ ✣ ✣

Nemah talks

As the boxes empty, Nemah talks to her Self.
Stores the words she needs Inside, throws the rest away.
After some time, she has emptied the last box.
The garbage bags are full,
the boxes
are all empty.

✣ ✣ ✣

Doctor grimaces through

"It's over now," she tells the doctor.

Doctor grimaces through their cigarette smoke, furls his brow, unfurls it. His curly rusted beard bends.

"Your hair looks good," he nods.

"It's just hair. I feel so blank," Nemah says. "What do I do now? What happens next?"

"Letting go," he says.

"How?" she asks.

"Do you have a lover?" he asks. "Did you find a woman?"

"No woman and no man," she says. "I have nothing left to give, nothing to share. I think there is no Me to spare."

"Why didn't you call me when you got out of rehab?" he asks. He looks at the telephone box on his desk, not at Nemah.

Nemah looks too.

"You wouldn't give me back my pills," she says. The phone box does not blink.

"Was that the only thing you needed?" he asks.

"I couldn't think of anything else," she says.

"Words," he says.

"Too many words. I am so tired of it . . . doctors and hospitals, sex and family, the taking away of . . . I am so very tired. It should be over now. I never should have lived," she says.

"At all?"

"This long." Nemah twists her bare spring toes around the chair leg. "It is too long, I feel too old to start again. Too empty. I know too much. But I know nothing. After all this, I still know nothing. How to start over, how to piece it all together."

"There will be something," the doctor says.

"I don't know," says Nemah. "Some reason for all this life, I don't think so."

Doctor nods quizzically at Nemah's toes. She glances and grimaces too. With an ache deeper than bone, Nemah rises from this doctor's chair, untangles herself from this tired room too full of empty words.

"I have to go now, it's time," she says.

✣ ✣ ✣

A time of grace

Swing, that swing with green spring grass and forest all around. The blind mother hanging laundry. A time of grace, a given moment.

She returns to it now in memory. Seat sliding on the smooth warm wooden slat, hemp rope firmly under tender palms, she jump-starts herself and pushes. Pushes away from that black dirt below, where the dead lie buried and silenced forever.

She pushes, pushes away the sandbox where she has built herself a tiny secret village. Real miniature people who live down there and move around up inside her brain.

✣ ✣ ✣

the bridge ahead

Nemah leaves the doctor, she feels a gnawing hollow growing inside her now.

That deep prairie sky bored into her soul hangs low, she cannot see it but it is part of her, she doesn't have to see it. Across the bridge ahead is the hospital and behind her is the doctor. The bridge has lumpy stone-grey edges. Rocks catch late spring sun and spray sparkles like precious metal. As a child, Nemah often picked pebbles—pebbles studded with mica to pull off in layers, the layers stuck on her fingertips, sparkling like diamonds.

River stretches as far north and south as she can see, the water calm and placid. On the riverbank are trees sprinkled with their first leaves. The river is an option, the water is one option. Nemah looks into it. Maybe a kid would find her body, some kid in innocence, in play. Some kid with a chance, some kid with a future.

This letting go is hard, it hurts.

She leaves the edge of the bridge, takes one last look. Hugs herself inside, scolds herself.

Here, in this city of bridges, too much has already been lost.

Across the bridge, facing the hospital, is a park. Spring-green and honey-dripping with new heat. Sunbathers, daycare kids, old people still cold from winter, watching. Kids scream, Nemah listens, they sound happy. Bird-words, a mother scolds her chicks, Nemah hears their raucous laughter.

"Hey lady! Gimme a push on this swing!"

Nemah sees a girl, maybe five, her face full of freckles. Sunsoaked already.

"You want a push on that swing?" she asks, getting closer. "Do you know how to pump your feet?"

The child nods vigorously and grins.

"See?" Her feet jut straight out from her body and then

abruptly convulse beneath her swing. She shows Nemah a few times. "I just can't get started by myself. Can you gimme a push?"

Nemah stands carefully behind her and begins to push gently.

"Like this?" asks Nemah.

"Harder!" the child urges and kicks her feet wildly.

Nemah pushes, feels the stride, mimics the rhythm. Braids flying, the girl rises high above Nemah. Nemah ducks to avoid the flailing legs above her.

Careful.

The girl is soaring now, keeping herself aloft.

"See how high I am!" she shouts. "No one can get me! I'm higher than God!"

Nemah leaves the flying, shouting girl-child. At the edge of the playground, she turns to watch her for a moment, making sure she's alright. Then she opens her bag. Inside, there is a pen, there is a fresh pad of lined paper.

She will return to the riverbank. She will sit on the warm spring grass, feel the heating sun. She will hear the children's shouts, she will breathe in air. She will write new words, she will make some sense of this knowledge that she has accumulated. She will take her truth where she can find it.

She will breathe in air.

LYNNETTE DUECK trained as a journalist and is the first single parent to graduate from the Creative Communications program at Winnipeg's Red River Community College. She wrote *sing me no more* during her final year in the program, in part to facilitate her self-healing and to validate her own experiences with abusive relationships and substance addiction.

Dueck has been a long-time advocate for reproductive rights and quality daycare, and has been actively involved with equality issues, especially those affecting the lives of single parent women and their children. She has been employed with the Saskatchewan Status of Women, the AIDS Saskatoon project, and Planned Parenthood. Her poetry, artwork, reviews, and editorials have been published in such publications as *Prairie Fire*, the *Mennonite Mirror*, and the *Winnipeg Sun*.

Lynnette Dueck currently lives in Winnipeg with her two children, Moses and Abra, her partner Brad, and their cats.

COLETTE LEISEN is a Vancouver-based artist who misses the "one-quarter land, three-quarters sky" landscape of Alberta, where she was born and lived for twenty-six years. After completing a degree in Education she relocated to Vancouver, where she became a self-taught photographer whose work has been exhibited in various galleries. She cares passionately about her art work, her role as an arts educator, and her involvement in human rights causes such as benefits for AIDS support groups and the Pro-Choice Women's Coalition. Colette would like to acknowledge the loving support she receives from her family and friends.

Press Gang Publishers Feminist Co-operative is committed to publishing a wide range of writing by women which explores themes of personal and political struggles for equality.

A free listing of our books is available from Press Gang Publishers, 603 Powell Street, Vancouver, B.C. V6A 1H2 Canada